J 818.209
HAR

S0-BNR-913

WALLINGFORD PUBLIC LIBRARY
200 North Main Street
Wallingford, CT 06492

Famous
Legends

The Legend of
Rip Van Winkle

WALLINGFORD PUBLIC LIBRARY
CHILDREN'S LIBRARY

By
Mark Harasymiw

Gareth Stevens
PUBLISHING

Please visit our website, www.garethstevens.com. For a free color catalog of all our high-quality books, call toll free 1-800-542-2595 or fax 1-877-542-2596.

Library of Congress Cataloging-in-Publication Data

Harasymiw, Mark.
The legend of Rip Van Winkle / by Mark Harasymiw.
p. cm. — (Famous Legends)
Includes index.
ISBN 978-1-4824-2744-8 (pbk.)
ISBN 978-1-4824-2745-5 (6 pack)
ISBN 978-1-4824-2746-2 (library binding)
1. Van Winkle, Rip (Fictitious character) — Juvenile fiction. 2. Irving, Washington, 1783-1859 — Juvenile literature. I. Harasymiw, Mark. II. Title.
PS2068.H35 2016
818'.209-d23

First Edition

Published in 2016 by
Gareth Stevens Publishing
111 East 14th Street, Suite 349
New York, NY 10003

Copyright © 2016 Gareth Stevens Publishing

Designer: Laura Bowen
Editor: Therese Shea

Photo credits: Cover, p. 1 Transcendental Graphics/Archive Photos/Getty Images; cover, p. 1 (ribbon) barbaliss/ Shutterstock.com; cover, p. 1 (leather) Pink Pueblo/Shutterstock.com; cover, pp. 1–32 (sign) Sarawut Padungkwan/ Shutterstock.com; cover, pp. 1–32 (vines) vitasunny/Shutterstock.com; cover, pp. 1–32 (parchment) TyBy/ Shutterstock.com; cover, pp. 1–32 (background) HorenkO/Shutterstock.com; p. 5 (map) blinkblink/Shutterstock.com; p. 5 (inset) Henry Inman/Wikimedia Commons; p. 7 (main) Kim Carson/Photodisc/Getty Images; p. 7 (inset) Library of Congress/Wikimedia Commons; p. 9 N.C. Wyeth/Wikimedia Commons; p. 11 Universal History Archive/ Universal Images Group/Getty Images; p. 13 Omikron Omikron/Science Source/Getty Images; pp. 15, 19 (inset) Print Collector/Hulton Archive/Getty Images; p. 17 (main) Hulton Archive/Stringer/Getty Images; p. 17 (inset) Mazbin/ Wikimedia Commons; pp. 19 (main), 21 (main) Universal Images Group/Getty Images; p. 21 (inset) Gilbert Stuart/ Wikimedia Commons; p. 23 (main) Randolph Caldecott/Wikimedia Commons; p. 23 (inset) Khutuck Bot/Wikimedia Commons; p. 25 (main) MyLoupe/Universal Images Group/Getty Images; p. 25 (inset) Soerfm/Wikimedia Commons; p. 27 Ted Spiegel/National Geographic/Getty Images; p. 29 (main) Mathew Brady/Wikimedia Commons; p. 29 (inset) John Greim/LightRocket/Getty Images.

All rights reserved. No part of this book may be reproduced in any form without permission in writing from the publisher, except by a reviewer.

Printed in the United States of America

CPSIA compliance information: Batch #CS15GS: For further information contact Gareth Stevens, New York, New York at 1-800-542-2595.

Contents

Words in the glossary appear in **bold** type the first time they are used in the text.

American Legend

"Rip Van Winkle" was one of the first famous American stories. Washington Irving, its author, was one of the first famous American writers.

The short story begins in New York when it was still one of the British colonies. George III was then king of England as well as the 13 colonies. Irving wrote that his main character, Rip Van Winkle, came from a Dutch family who settled in North America. Though Rip's **ancestors** were great soldiers, he wasn't like them at all.

The Inside Story

The Dutch began a North American colony called New Netherland in 1621. The British took it over in 1664 and renamed it New York.

New York State

Hudson River valley

Catskills

The short story "Rip Van Winkle" was said to have taken place in the Catskill Mountains and Hudson River valley, real places in New York State.

5

Who Was Rip Van Winkle?

Rip Van Winkle was a "simple good-natured man." He was popular with the children of his village. He played with them and told them stories. He loved taking long walks to go hunting or fishing. He would never refuse to help out a neighbor, even with very hard work.

However, Rip found it impossible to do his own work. He just didn't enjoy laboring on his farm or making money for himself. So, Rip and his family were quite poor.

The Inside Story

Washington Irving described the Catskill Mountains, a setting in "Rip Van Winkle," as having a "magical hue."

Washington Irving wrote that Rip Van Winkle's village was at the foot of the "Kaatskill Mountains," or today's Catskill Mountains.

Rip Van Winkle

7

Dame Van Winkle

The Van Winkle farm was in bad shape. The fences were falling apart, and weeds grew everywhere. The family was usually dressed in ragged clothes. Rip didn't mind this. He enjoyed his life and the people in it, except for one person—his wife.

Dame Van Winkle wasn't happy with Rip. She would yell at him morning, noon, and night about his easygoing ways. Rip wouldn't answer her. He'd shake his head. When she became very upset, he'd stand and leave the house silently. His faithful dog, Wolf, would follow him.

In the story, Rip's wife complained about "his **idleness**, his carelessness, and the ruin he was bringing on his family."

9

Strange Sights

One day, Rip's wife nagged him about his faults until he escaped to go hunting with Wolf. After walking for some time, Rip sat down to rest. While he was sitting there, he heard his name being called.

Rip saw a man carrying a barrel on his back. The strange-looking man asked Rip for help. They walked a long way together until they came across a group of men. The men were playing ninepins, a bowling game! After a while, Rip helped himself to the strong drink in the man's barrel. He soon fell asleep.

The Inside Story

Rip said the ninepin balls sounded like thunder in the mountains.

Rip noticed the men he met in the mountains were dressed in old-fashioned clothing. They reminded him of men he saw in an old painting.

11

A Long Nap

When Rip Van Winkle awoke, it was morning. He wasn't in the grass-covered clearing where he had first fallen asleep. That was strange, but he didn't think much about it. He knew he'd slept a lot longer than he had meant to. He had to get home. His wife would be angry.

Rip called for his dog, but Wolf didn't come. He must be lost in the forest, Rip thought. He didn't want to wait for Wolf. He began to walk to the village.

The Inside Story

Rip looked for his gun when he woke up. The only gun he found was very rusty, so he didn't think it was his.

There are many images of Rip Van Winkle waking up for the first time after his magical sleep.

13

Homecoming

In the village, Rip saw people he didn't know. They were dressed strangely. He came upon his house and discovered it had fallen apart! Rip wandered the town asking about his family. People thought he was crazy.

Finally, a woman explained to Rip that 20 years had passed since the day he went hunting. She was Rip's daughter! His son was still alive too, but Dame Van Winkle had died. Rip lived with his daughter after that. He enjoyed the rest of his life, taking walks and telling stories.

The Inside Story

An old man in the village said Rip must have met Henry Hudson, the first explorer of that area. Hudson and his men haunted the Catskills every 20 years!

Rip told the townspeople he was a loyal subject of King George. During the 20 years Rip slept, he missed the American Revolution, the war in which the colonies won their freedom from England!

15

Inspiration

Much of Irving's **inspiration** for "Rip Van Winkle" came from the German tale "Peter Klaus." Peter took care of goats in the country. One day, Peter's goats began to go missing. One by one, they were walking through a hole in a wall. Peter, too, went through the hole. He found knights playing ninepins on the other side. He drank their wine and fell asleep.

When Peter awoke and went home, he found much had changed. Many of the people in his village were strangers, except for his daughter—who was now 20 years older!

In the tale, Peter Klaus is said to live near Kyffhäuser Mountain in Germany. A picture of Kyffhäuser as it appears today is below.

Changing a Legend

"Rip Van Winkle" is much like "Peter Klaus." However, Washington Irving made changes so that Rip was more likable and the story more exciting.

In the original tale, Peter was a goatherder who hated to do work. Rip didn't mind working to help out others. "Rip Van Winkle" also seems a bit more magical. Readers are supposed to think the ghosts of Henry Hudson and his sailors had something to do with Rip's long sleep. However, there's no reason given for Peter's 20-year nap.

The Inside Story

Another well-known Washington Irving short story was "The Legend of Sleepy Hollow." This spooky tale, published with "Rip Van Winkle," also took place in the Hudson River valley.

In Rip's tale, the ninepin bowlers were men who explored America. Peter's bowlers were German knights (right).

Meet Washington Irving

Washington Irving was born on April 3, 1783, in New York City. He was the 11th and youngest child in his family. Although he wasn't the best student, he loved to read. He read adventure stories in school, hiding his books under his desk.

Irving later trained as a lawyer, but didn't enjoy learning about the law or being a lawyer. So, he began a writing **career** in 1802. He wrote **essays** under another name: "Jonathan Oldstyle."

The Inside Story

Washington Irving was named after George Washington.

Washington Irving (left) met George Washington at a shop in New York City when Irving was 6 years old!

Internationally Famous

Like the law, the Irving family's **import** business didn't hold Washington Irving's interest. He worked for his family from time to time, but his true love was writing.

In 1815, Irving traveled to England to work in his family's office. While there, he published *The Sketch Book* in 1819 and 1820. It was a collection of essays and stories, some factual and some make-believe. It sold so well in the United States and England that he could finally earn a living as a writer.

The Inside Story

The full name of *The Sketch Book* was *The Sketch Book of Geoffrey Crayon, Gent.* "Geoffrey Crayon" was another of Washington Irving's pen names.

This is a picture from another story in *The Sketch Book* called "Christmas Dinner." It was created by famous British artist Randolph Caldecott.

THE

SKETCH BOOK

OF

GEOFFREY CRAYON, Gent.

No. I.

"I have no wife nor children, good or bad, to provide for. A mere spectator of other men's fortunes and adventures, and how they play their parts; which methinks are diversely presented unto me, as from a common theatre or scene."

BURTON.

NEW-YORK:

PRINTED BY C. S. VAN WINKLE,
101 Greenwich Street.
....
1819.

Traveling and Writing

Irving traveled and wrote for several years. He lived in Spain from 1826 to 1829. Irving published the book *Life and Voyages of Columbus* in 1828. In the mid-1800s, it was the most commonly owned book in American libraries!

In Spain, Irving also wrote a collection of Spanish stories called *The Alhambra*. Published in 1832, it contained tales he learned from a young Spanish man named Mateo Ximenes.

Between 1829 and 1832, Irving worked for the US government in England. He worked with future US president Martin Van Buren there.

A statue of Washington Irving stands on the grounds of the Alhambra palace in Spain (below).

25

At Home at Sunnyside

Washington Irving returned to the United States in 1832. He bought a beautiful home in Tarrytown, New York, that he called Sunnyside.

Irving was soon hired by John Jacob Astor, one of the richest men in America, to write the **biography** of Astor's fur-trading adventures. Called *Astoria*, it was published in 1836.

One of Irving's last works was a five-book biography of George Washington's life. Soon after he finished his *Life of Washington*, Irving died on November 28, 1859.

The Inside Story

In 1842, Charles Dickens visited Washington Irving at Sunnyside. Dickens was the author of the stories *Oliver Twist* and *A Christmas Carol*.

Sunnyside was Washington Irving's home in Tarrytown, New York, near the Hudson River. "It is a beautiful spot," Irving wrote, "capable of being made a little paradise."

Legacy

Washington Irving may not be as well known today, but 100 years ago, both he and his works were famous in both the United States and Europe. *The Sketch Book* was considered the first American book to become an international success.

Many Europeans at the time thought the United States was filled with simple or wild people. "Rip Van Winkle" and Irving's other works showed people around the world that the young nation already had a rich **culture**. And much more great American writing was to come.

Washington Irving was buried in Sleepy Hollow, New York. This was the setting of the story "The Legend of Sleepy Hollow."

Glossary

ancestor: a relative who lived long before you

biography: a book about someone's life written by another person

career: the job someone chooses to do for a long time

culture: the beliefs and ways of life of a group of people

essay: a piece of writing

hue: appearance

idleness: laziness

import: to bring in goods from another country

inspiration: something that makes someone want to do something or that gives someone an idea about what to do or create

publish: to produce material in print for sale

For More Information

Books

Harness, Cheryl. *The Literary Adventures of Washington Irving: American Storyteller.* Washington DC: National Geographic, 2008.

Irving, Washington. *The Legend of Sleepy Hollow and Other Stories.* Mankato, MN: Creative Education, 2011.

Irving, Washington. *Rip Van Winkle.* Mankato, MN: Creative Education, 2011.

Websites

Rip Van Winkle
archive.org/stream/ripvanwinkle00irvi#page/n0/mode/2up
Read the complete "Rip Van Winkle" story online.

Washington Irving's Sunnyside
www.hudsonvalley.org/historic-sites/washington-irvings-sunnyside
See pictures and read about Washington Irving's home at Sunnyside.

Publisher's note to educators and parents: Our editors have carefully reviewed these websites to ensure that they are suitable for students. Many websites change frequently, however, and we cannot guarantee that a site's future contents will continue to meet our high standards of quality and educational value. Be advised that students should be closely supervised whenever they access the Internet.

Index

A 2170 735300 5